ST. MARY SCHOOL
LIBRARY

DATE DUE

NOV 2 1 1995			
NOV 2 8 1995			

F
ABE

#2 copy   '95-157

mystery
DEMCO

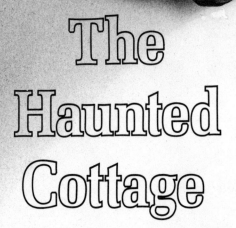

The
Haunted
Cottage

By Harriette Sheffer Abels

Illustrated by Joann Daley

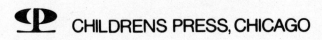

CHILDRENS PRESS, CHICAGO

For my children
Barbara, David, and Carol

Library of Congress Cataloging in Publication Data

Abels, Harriette Scheffer.
  The haunted cottage.

  SUMMARY: The peace of a family's retreat to an
isolated mountain cottage is shattered when a ghost
makes its presence known.
  [1. Ghost stories] I. Daley, Joann. II. Title.
PZ7.A1595Hau   [Fic]   77-16619
ISBN 0-516-03486-3

  2 3 4 5 6 7 8 9 10 11 12 R 85 84 83 82 81 80 79

The
Haunted
Cottage

CHAPTER ONE

The car pulled into the driveway of the deserted cottage. Danny Russo got out and stretched his arms wide. It had been a long ride from the city to this small town in the mountains.

"Hey, Dan! Look!" His younger brother Pete pointed to a narrow path. It led down a steep hill to a clear blue lake below.

"Super!" Danny could almost feel the cool water lapping over his bare feet.

He turned to his parents, who were busy emptying the car. "I wonder why nobody ever rented this cottage before. It looks terrific."

"Lend a hand here, Danny," his father said. He handed him a pile of blankets. "I don't know why this place has been empty so long. Nine years, the agent told me. Maybe it's too far from the lake."

Danny's mother unlocked the front door and they went into the cottage. The afternoon sun streamed through the front windows. It was a light, cheerful-looking house.

Danny dropped the blankets he was carrying. "Come on, Pete. Let's explore."

They ran upstairs and glanced quickly through the three bedrooms. He and Pete would sleep in one and his parents in another. The third his father would use as an office. He was writing a book that he hoped to finish this summer.

The boys helped unload the groceries in the kitchen and then went upstairs to unpack their clothes. When the suitcases were empty they took them downstairs.

"There's a storage shed behind the house," their father said. "Put the suitcases in there."

Danny picked up the two big cases and left the smaller ones for Pete. They went out through the kitchen door to the back of the house.

There was a small building built onto the back of the kitchen. An old red maple tree threw its shadow across

the whitewashed brick walls. There was a lock on the wooden door.

Danny got the key from his mother and opened the shed door.

As he stepped through the doorway, a blast of cold air hit him in the face. It sent a chill through his whole body.

"Whew!" he muttered. "This place must have been locked up for the whole nine years." He set the suitcases down in a corner and turned to take the ones Pete was carrying.

Pete was standing behind him, his face as pale as milk.

"What's the matter?" Danny asked. "Are you sick?"

Pete shook his head. His skinny fingers clutched the two bags tightly to his sides. "I feel funny in here—as if something cold is crawling all over me."

Danny laughed. "Okay, give me the bags. We'll get out of here."

But Pete stood frozen, and Danny finally had to pull the suitcases away from him.

"What happened to you?" he asked when they were outside again.

Pete looked down at the ground and shrugged. "Nothing. It was kind of creepy in there and it got to me."

Danny nodded. "Yeah, that's because it's been locked up for so long. Don't worry about it." He knocked Pete playfully on the shoulder.

His mother fixed a quick dinner and after they had eaten, they went up to bed. It was still early but the long drive had tired them all out.

CHAPTER TWO

Danny got into his bed and curled up to go to sleep. He heard Pete turn off the light as he was dozing off.

He was almost asleep when he heard the tapping. His father must have started work on his book right away. But he wished he'd close the office door so they wouldn't hear the typewriter. He stuck his head under the pillow and tried to ignore the sound. But now it seemed louder than ever. He sat up in bed, suddenly wide awake.

"Do you hear it too, Danny?" Pete whispered from the other bed.

"Do you mean Dad's typewriter? Sure I hear it. How could I miss it?" Danny's eyes were accustomed to the dark now. He saw Pete sitting up in his bed, clutching the sheet to his chin.

"That isn't the typewriter," Pete said. "It's coming from downstairs."

Danny slid out of the bed. "Then it must be Mom in the kitchen." He went out into the hall. Everything downstairs was dark. He could hear the tapping clearly.

"Is it Mom?" Pete had crept up behind him.

A light went on in the other bedroom. "Boys?" It was their mother calling. "What are you doing out there?"

They went into their parent's room. Both of them were in bed and had obviously been asleep.

"There's something tapping downstairs," Danny said. "We thought you were doing something in the kitchen."

His father got out of bed. "Probably a window shade flapping. I'll fix it."

He went downstairs and Danny and Pete followed. The tapping had stopped.

His father glanced around. "I. don't know what you boys heard. You must have been dreaming."

"Both of us at the same time?" Pete looked at him, his eyes wide open.

His father laughed. "Okay, you weren't dreaming. But you can see for yourselves there's nothing here. Let's get to bed."

They went back up and Danny got into his bed. He slipped under the sheet.

The tapping started again. It was louder and clearer this time. It sounded as though it was coming from outside the front door.

"It's a cane!" Danny exclaimed. "It sounds like someone with a cane is coming up the front walk!"

He dashed into his father's room. "I can hear a cane on the brick walk," he said.

His father grabbed a flashlight and ran downstairs.

Danny could hear the tapping clearly until his father wrenched open the front door. Then it stopped.

His father beamed the flashlight down the front path. It was empty. He moved it quickly through the bushes that lined the walk, then skimmed it across the front yard. There was nothing.

His father slammed the door and locked it. "Are you satisfied? Now can I get some sleep?"

Danny stared at him. "Didn't you hear it when we were coming down the stairs?"

"Of course not." His father paused. "Well, I did hear some kind of a noise. But it was probably a squirrel on the roof. Or a cat roaming around. Now go to bed."

Danny went back to his room. Pete was sitting on his bed hugging his knees.

"Danny." Pete's voice sounded strange. "Do you think it could be a ghost?"

Danny snickered. "Where did you get a dumb idea like that?"

"Why hasn't anyone lived here for nine years? It's a nice house. Why didn't anyone ever rent it before?" Pete had come over to sit at Danny's feet. "Maybe somebody else did rent it but the ghost scared them off."

"Wow, you've been reading too many books." Danny slid down in the bed. "Dad is right. Go to sleep."

He didn't feel as tired as when he had first come to bed. He thought about Pete's theory that it was a ghost. He didn't believe in such things. He knew they didn't exist. Still, that sure had been a strange sound he had heard. And he didn't think it was a cat or a squirrel!

He sighed and closed his eyes. He would think about it some more tomorrow.

He had just dozed off when he heard a muffled thud. It sounded as if a book had fallen off the table.

"Danny!" Pete hissed at him from the other bed. "What was that?"

"A book dropped," Danny murmured. He wished Pete would go to sleep and leave him alone.

Pete was back on his bed. "There aren't any books in here. We haven't unpacked them yet."

Danny jumped up, wide awake for the second time. He turned on the light. "There must have been some books here before we came." He looked around the room. It was bare except for the clothes they had dropped here and there earlier that night.

"That book is here someplace," he muttered. "I heard it drop." He stopped and looked at Pete. "Are you playing a joke on me?"

But he knew before he said it that it wasn't true. His brother's face had that same white look it had had in the shed that afternoon. Pete was frightened!

Danny felt a sudden prickle of fear. There was something very strange about this cottage in the mountains.

He pushed his bed and Pete's together. "We'd better get some sleep," he said. "We'll tell Dad about this in the morning."

They settled down once again. This time the cottage stayed quiet. In a little while they were both sleeping soundly.

CHAPTER THREE

The next morning at breakfast their father laughed at their story. "Ghosts?" he snorted. "That's a good one. I thought you kids today were too smart to believe in that sort of stuff."

"I'm not a kid, but I believe in them," their mother said. Her expression was serious as she looked at her husband. "I'm not sure I believe they are the spirits of dead people. But I do believe that there are things that happen in this world that can't be explained away."

"I'll believe it when I see one." Their father drank the last of his coffee. "Next time he drops around, introduce me." He winked at Danny and Pete and left the room.

Danny looked intently at his mother. "Were you serious, Mom?"

"Yes." She nodded her head. "I've never met a ghost personally, but I know people who have. And they aren't weird people. They are people whose opinion I respect. I've never looked into it very deeply. But I do think there are things we know nothing about."

On and off during the day, Danny thought about what his mother had said. He'd never thought about ghosts seriously either. But he was going to now. Maybe he would find out that the things that had happened last night had a simple, logical explanation. But somehow he didn't think that was true.

By the time evening came, he had almost forgotten about the ghost. They had gone swimming in the lake in the afternoon and the water and hot sun had made him sleepy.

He tossed a Frisbee with Pete on the front lawn until it got dark. As they went into the house, Danny yawned. "Let's go to bed now and get up early. We can spend the whole day at the lake."

Pete agreed and they went up ahead of their parents.

Danny fell asleep right away. He was dreaming of being out on the lake on a raft when a sudden breeze made him shiver. His dream began to change as he got cooler and cooler in the breeze. He thought he was in a storm on the lake when he realized he was dreaming. He woke up with a start.

The room was cold. A stiff breeze was blowing through the open window. He could hear newspapers being blown across the floor. There must be a bad storm brewing.

"Danny, are you up?" Pete sounded as if he was almost crying.

Danny reached out and grabbed his shoulder. "Yeah, I'm right here. Don't be upset, it's only a summer storm. Listen to those papers rattle!"

Pete did start to cry. "That's why I'm scared. There aren't any papers in here!"

Danny gulped and stared into the dark. Pete was right. There were no newspapers in their room. In fact, there weren't any in the whole house! But he could hear them skittering along the floor!

He jumped out of bed and switched on the light. The noise stopped. The floor was bare. There was no paper of any kind in the room. He looked under the beds. There was nothing there.

"Danny. The wind has stopped!"

Danny ran to the window and looked out. The stars gleamed brightly in the sky. There wasn't a sign of a storm coming. A gentle breeze drifted into the room.

Danny shivered. He wondered if his father would blame this on a cat or a squirrel!

When he told his parents the story the next morning, they said they hadn't heard a thing.

"Look, guys. I believe you." His father was serious as they discussed what had happened. "I can see you both had a bad fright. But you mustn't blame it on ghosts. Believe me, there aren't any such things as ghosts."

His mother choked back a small laugh.

His father shot her a disgusted look. "Next time something happens, if there is a next time, wake me up. I'll find out right away what it is."

"Like you did the tapping on the sidewalk?" Danny asked.

His father was suddenly angry. "Don't get smart. And if this whole thing is a trick you boys are playing, you'd better cut it out very quickly!" He stomped out of the room and up to his office.

That night, as they were on their way to bed, he stopped them on the stairs. "I'm sorry I was angry this

morning," he said. "I just don't want you believing all
this ghost nonsense. If you hear anything tonight, call
me. Okay?"

"Sure." Danny and Pete went on up to their room.

CHAPTER FOUR

They were lying in the dark talking over the mysterious happenings, when they heard their parents come upstairs. Their mother stuck her head in the doorway and said good night. In a little while the house was quiet except for their own whispering.

The clicking noise had been going on for some time before Danny realized it.

He grabbed Pete's arm. "Listen!" He leaped out of bed. "I'm going to get Dad."

He rushed into his parent's room and found them sitting up in bed. "Dad," he began, "there's a strange . . ."

"I know," his father interrupted. "We hear it." He got up and got his flashlight. "It sounds as if it might be a cricket trapped in the house."

"No it doesn't." His mother's quiet voice came from the bed. "It doesn't sound like that at all."

His father switched on the light next to the bed. "Then what does it sound like?" he demanded angrily.

"Shh." She listened for a moment. "I'm not sure. But it's a familiar sound."

"I know!" Danny had suddenly recognized it. "It sounds like the click when you change slides in the projector!"

"Yes!" his mother agreed eagerly. "That's exactly what it sounds like."

His father went out and looked down the dark stairwell. "I wonder if someone got in and is fooling around with our stuff."

He switched on the hall light and went down with Danny behind him. There was no one downstairs. All the doors and windows were still locked from the inside.

"Dad, listen." Danny stood still. "It's following us. Every time we go into a room, the sound goes with us." He stared at his father. The familiar chill began to steal over him.

His father walked quietly into the kitchen. He came back to the hall and went across to the living room. He

walked up the stairs and into each of the three bedrooms. Everywhere he went, the sound followed.

"Now do you believe the boys?" His mother had gotten up and put her robe on. She had followed his father around the upper floor.

His father took a deep breath. "It certainly is strange. The only logical explanation I can think of is that a cricket is trapped in the walls."

"Oh, you and your crickets," his mother said. She went back into her room and got into bed.

"Go to sleep, boys. I'm sure it isn't anything. We'll be able to explain it all in the morning." He smiled and patted Pete on the head.

But Danny noticed the worried frown that creased his forehead. And he saw how slowly he went back into his own room, as if he were deep in thought.

The next night the noise started early. They were no sooner in bed than Danny heard the sound of the front door opening.

He had watched his father bolt and lock that door before they came upstairs. He ran to his parent's room but his father was already up and heading for the hall. He had heard the door, too.

They stood together at the head of the stairs.

"Someone is walking around down there," Danny whispered. He could hear the sound of leather heels clacking on the wooden floors.

"Who is there?" his father shouted. "What are you doing down there?"

He started down the steps.

"Dad, don't!" Danny cried. "Call the police."

But his father continued on down, holding the flashlight tightly gripped in his hand as if it were a weapon.

Danny followed behind him.

When they reached the front hall, the footsteps stopped. They searched the whole lower floor but there was no sign of an intruder.

"This is crazy," his father said. "All the doors are locked. The windows are closed. No one could have come in. But I hear someone walking around. Well, if anyone was here, he's gone now."

But he wasn't gone. As soon as they were back upstairs, the footsteps started again. Four times they raced up and down the stairway. Each time the sound stopped as soon as they were downstairs.

"You know, Pete," his father said after the fourth trip, "I'm beginning to believe your theory about ghosts."

"It isn't a theory," Pete declared. "Danny believes it. Mom believes it. You're the only one who thinks I'm crazy."

His father grinned at him. "You aren't crazy. But I wish I knew what your ghost wants from us. I wish he'd let us get one good night's sleep."

"He probably wants us out of his house," his mother said. "Maybe he likes living alone."

Danny laughed along with the others, but another thought suddenly came to him. "Maybe he's trying to tell us something. The other people who stayed here probably left before he could get through to them. But we seem to hear him more clearly all the time."

His father thought over what he had said. "But none of the things that have happened have any connection," he said. "They are just strange events and noises."

"I have noticed one thing about the noises," his mother said slowly. "They always seem to move toward the kitchen."

Danny jumped up. "You're right." He ran down to the kitchen. He hadn't taken a really good look at the room since they had arrived.

He switched on the overhead light and looked around. It seemed to be a perfectly ordinary kitchen.

The others had followed him downstairs. "What is that door over there?" he asked his mother.

"It's locked and I haven't bothered to open it," she said. "I assume it leads to that shed out back. It's in the right spot."

"And we know there isn't anything in there," Danny said. "It was empty when Pete and I went in."

Pete shivered. "It was cold. And it was creepy."

His father herded them all back upstairs. "If the ghost wants to walk all night, he can. We're going to sleep."

There wasn't another sound the rest of the night.

CHAPTER FIVE

The next day Danny decided to hang around the house.

"How come?" Pete asked him.

Danny drew him out behind the house. They sat under the old red maple. "I want to know whether things happen in the daylight or whether he always waits until after dark. Maybe things have been going on and we've missed them because we were down at the lake."

Pete agreed that it was a good idea. But it was a total waste. There wasn't one creak or footstep or breeze all day that wasn't real.

That night at supper Danny's father said he had to go back to the city for a few days. "Will you three be all right here while I'm gone?" he asked. "I hate to leave you with our mysterious friend."

"Don't be silly," his mother said. "He's spooky, but we know he can't hurt us. Maybe while you're gone he will be able to get his message through."

After dinner Danny's father sent him out to the shed to get one of the small suitcases.

"Do you want me to go with you, Dan?" Pete asked.

Danny laughed. "No thanks. With all that has been going on around here, I'm not afraid of a little cold. And you hate that place."

Pete shuddered. "I sure do."

Danny took the key and went around the back. He opened the shed door and reached for the light switch.

He screamed in terror. The room was filled with moths! Fluttering, flapping, swirling . . . they blew through the small room in a gigantic whirlwind. Danny threw his hands up in front of his face. They were in his hair, his eyes, his ears, his mouth.

He turned and stumbled blindly out the door. As soon as he was outside he ran screaming for his father. He sobbed out the story of what had happened and his father dashed out to the shed.

He came back in a few minutes. "Danny, come with me."

"I can't. Please, Dad. Don't make me." His heart was still pounding from the fright of the attack.

His father's voice was quiet. "Danny, there aren't any moths in there. There isn't a sign of any ever having been there."

Danny was stunned. He ran out to the shed and peered into the little room. It looked exactly as he and Pete had left it a few days before. There were no moths, dead or alive.

He spun around. His parents and Pete had followed him out. "Dad, I don't . . ." he stumbled over his words. "I know they were . . ."

"I believe you," his father interrupted. "I'm not saying you didn't tell the truth. But I think we have to reconsider my leaving you here with your mother and brother. It seems it isn't true that the ghost can't hurt you."

His mother leaned up against the old red maple. "Now what?" she asked.

"Now we get out of here," his father said. "This isn't funny anymore. We'll go see that agent in the morning and get our money back. There must be other cottages around here that aren't rented."

A few raindrops fell on the back of Danny's neck. "Hey," he said, it's starting to sprinkle."

They went inside and in a few minutes a light summer shower had started.

"We'll get a good night's sleep," his mother said, "and we'll move first thing in the morning."

Danny and Pete were already in bed when the storm broke. Flashes of lightning streaked through the sky. Thunder roared and pounded overhead.

"Why is it so loud?" Pete asked. He sounded scared.

"Because we're in the mountains," Danny said. "It's always louder up here. I guess it's because the air is clearer." He wasn't sure that was true. He said it only to keep Pete calm.

42

Suddenly, there was a loud crash and the whole house shook.

"What was that?" Pete started to cry.

Danny heard his father's footsteps pounding down the hall. "What was it, Dad? Did the lightning hit the house?"

"It hit something," his father yelled as he dashed down the stairs.

Danny raced down after him. They ran out the front door into the heavy rain. It wasn't until they got to the backyard that they saw what had happened.

The old red maple had been hit by the lightning. It had toppled over onto the shed. The roof of the shed had collapsed and two of the brick walls were knocked flat.

Danny walked over to take a closer look. Suddenly, he cried out.

"Dad—quick—look!" He pointed to the place where the wall had fallen away from the cement floor.

The bony skeleton of a human arm stuck straight up through the debris.

His father threw his arm around his shoulders and held him close.

"Now we know what our ghost has been trying to tell us." He sighed and turned away. "We'd better go call the police."

They walked slowly across the wet grass and went into the quiet cottage.

Though the ending of this book is fictional, the events described in *The Haunted Cottage* were observed by a college professor and his wife at a cottage on Cape Cod, Massachusetts. The professor told the story in an article written for *Harper's Magazine*, November, 1934, entitled *Four Months in a Haunted House*. The story is printed in *Unbidden Guests: A Book of Real Ghosts*, by William O. Stevens, published by Dodd, Mead & Co., Inc., 1945, 1946, 1956.

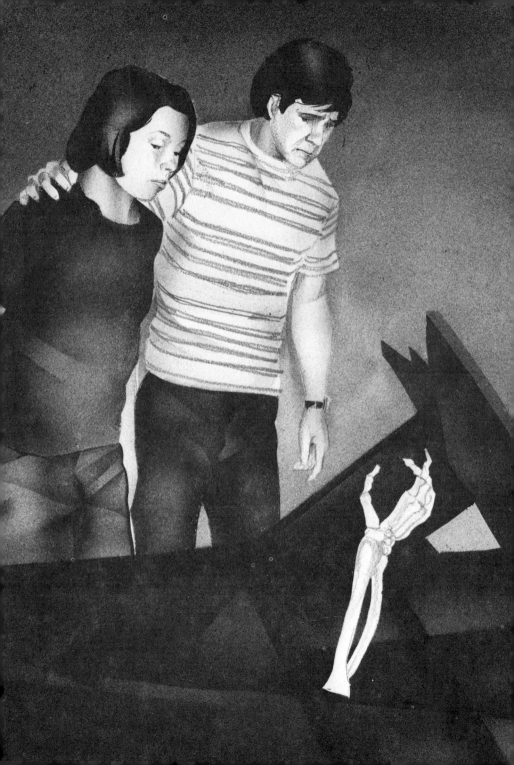

About the Author

Harriette Sheffer Abels was born in Port Chester, New York. She attended Furman University in Greenville, South Carolina for one year. During that year her poetry was published in the Furman literary magazine and she wrote, produced, and directed a three-act musical comedy for the freshman skit. She came to California in 1946, and began writing in 1963. Her stories and books have been published continuously since her first sale in 1964. Mrs. Abels doesn't have a lot of time for writing, but she does some writing every day at an old English school desk in her breakfast room. Her typewriter and other writing materials are kept in the service porch. She is a member of the Lunch Bunch, a very professional group of ten "housewives who write." In six years members of the group have published ninety books and three or four hundred articles and stories. Mrs. Abels and her husband, Robert Hamilton Abels, have three grown children and three dogs. They love to travel and have taken many trips to Europe.

About the Artist

Joann Daley attended the Society of Arts and Crafts in Detroit before making Chicago her home. She has established herself as a highly sought after illustrator, working on both agency and editorial accounts. She has recently joined with Pencil Point Studio in South Haven, Michigan as a freelance illustrator, thus expanding her market. In her spare time Joann likes to paint.